To Odysseus—the next generation.

—L.M.

I dedicate this book to my very young sons, Kelley and Cameron, and the promise and possibilities in them.

I also dedicate it to my husband and their dad, Vincent, who has a way of making everything new

look easy and fun. And, dear reader, it's dedicated to the music in you. May you play it with gusto.

—Sincerely, D.C.B.

345 Hudson Street, New York, NY 10014. G. P. Putnam's Sons, Reg. U.S. Pat. & Tm. Off. Published simultaneously in Canada. Printed in Hong Kong by South China
Printing Co. (1988) Ltd. Designed by Sharon Jacobs. Text set in nineteen-point Elroy. Library of Congress Cataloging-in-Publication Data Moss, Lloyd.
Our marching band / by Lloyd Moss ; illustrated by Diana Cain Bluthenthal.   p. cm.   Summary: When all the girls and boys in the neighborhood take up musical
instruments, at first they produce awful tones, but after much practice they are able to come together as a marching band that brings brassy, classy fun.
ISBN 0-399-23335-0   [1. Marching bands Fiction. 2. Bands (Music) Fiction. 3. Musical instruments Fiction. 4. Stories in rhyme.]   I. Bluthenthal, Diana Cain, ill.
II. Title. PZ8.3. M84640u 2001   [E]—dc21   99-37284   10 9 8 7 6 5 4 3 2 1   First Impression

OUR MARCHING BAND

Lloyd Moss

ILLUSTRATED BY

Diana Cain Bluthenthal

G. P. Putnam's Sons • New York

A neighbor boy, Mel Mackelroy,

Had seriously planned

To learn to play the trumpet

And go marching in a band.

Belinda Blore, who lived next door,

Decided on her own,

She'd go parading, serenading

On a slide trombone.

Across the street, Maureen Magritte thought,

"Wouldn't it be cute

To wear a fancy uniform

And tootle on a flute!"

Around the corner, Harry Horner

Had his mind all set:

He'd soon be taking lessons,

And would learn the clarinet.

One house away, Shavaun O'Shea,

In mapping out her life,

Had planned to blow a piccolo

(Which some folks call a fife),

And down the block, Ralph Rosenstock

Made up his mind to play

A tuba or a sousaphone,

Whichever came his way.

To Calvin Crum, to beat a drum
Held marvelous appeal,

While Betsy Brown would go to town
Upon a glockenspiel.

Sam Saks would own a saxophone
He'd learn to play upon,

And Mae McCall would lead them all
By twirling a baton.

The kids agreed they had the need

To practice every day.

For blocks around there came the sound

Of instruments at play.

Throughout the start, each person's part

Just didn't sound too good;

The girls and boys produced a noise

That stunned the neighborhood.

The grown-ups groaned,

And sighed and moaned.

They sobbed and tore their hair!

Those awful tones just shook their bones;

They came from everywhere.

"That sound annoys! It near destroys!"

They bellow and complain.

"Confound that noise!

Those girls and boys are driving us insane!"

But bit by bit, the sound of it

Got better by degrees,

And day by day, with practice,

Play had soon begun to please.

By never veering,

Persevering, early morn 'til late,

The hours spent in practice meant

They now were sounding great.

Town Mayor Bly went passing by
And cried, "What lovely sound!
It's simply grand, so close at hand,
This dandy band I've found!

"It's my intent they'll represent
The town, and I will try
To see they've played our big parade
The next Fourth of July!"

That day is here.

The way is clear.

They're standing in a line.

Their outfits grand befit the band;

Their instruments all shine.

The whistle blows.

They're on their toes.

Mae raises her baton.

Then down it comes!

A roll on drums

By Calvin means "March on!"

Mel's trumpet blare invades the air
With clear and sparkling tone.
Belinda blows, and music flows
In waves from her trombone.

Maureen is seen behind them
And her flute is trilling high,
And Harry lets his clarinet
Sing out while marching by.

Shavaun is on the piccolo,

Ralph's tuba booms with zeal,

Sam's sax extends its notes and blends

With Betsy's glockenspiel.

They march in style.

Just see them smile!

Their voices blend as one.

The crowds all cheer as they draw near.

What brassy, classy fun!

Their neighbors greet them on the street

And cry, "You sound so good!

When starting out, we had no doubt;

We always knew you would.

"Did you succeed? Yes! It indeed

Proceeded just as planned.

We're mighty proud! We'll shout out loud: